How to Catch Santa

BY JEAN REAGAN

ILLUSTRATED BY LEE WILDISH

ALFRED A. KNOPF 🐕 NEW YOKK

ISBN 978-0-375-97970-5

This special edition was printed for Kohl's Department Stores, Inc.
(for distribution on behalf of Kohl's Cares, LLC,
its wholly owned subsidiary)
by Penguin Random House LLC.

KOHL'S
Style: JHDI-4873
Factory Number: 208840
7/19

MANUFACTURED IN CHINA   10 9 8 7 6 5 4 3 2 1

Dear Santa,
I would like ...
- $ 20,000,000,000
- 1 shooting star
- spaceship
- Tiger
- New longer Arms

Carl

Dear Santa,
I would be very happy if you could bring me ...
a cloud.
or a Doll's house.
Thank you,
Tilly

Dear Santa,
I would like
a robot and
x-ray eyes for
Christmas please
also if you have time
bionic legs....
Jerry

DEAR SANTA,
I would like
the best present
in the world...
please keep this
letter and reuse
for the next year!
Sam

Dear Santa,
anything but
Socks. thanks,
Dad

After waiting for days and days and *days*, it's finally
Christmas Eve.
　And *that's* when you can try to catch Santa.

As you know, Santa's very busy, and you won't be able to keep him for long. So plan ahead. Figure out *now* how to make the most of your time.

First of all, don't you have a zillion questions to ASK him?

QUESTIONS FOR SANTA:

How do you squeeze down chimneys?

How do you stay clean?

What about houses with no chimneys?

How fast do reindeer fly to get everywhere in one night?

What's their fuel? Magic?

Do elves ever sneak a ride in your sleigh?
What about kids?

How do you find kids who are away on trips?

What's *your* favorite toy?

Do you get mountains and **mountains** of letters?

Who invents new toys
at your workshop?

The elves?

Mrs. Claus?

You?

Do you really eat cookies at everyone's house?

Maybe you have things you want to TELL him.

THINGS TO TELL SANTA:

I'm trying very hard
to be good.
My sister is, too, even if it doesn't
look like it.

Thank you for the presents!
Sorry I always forget to send
a thank-you note.

I know what
my mom and dad want.
They were too busy to write to you.

And maybe you have things you want to GIVE him.
(Santa will *love* that!)

THINGS TO GIVE
SANTA:

A headlamp for going
down dark, dark chimneys

A nose warmer for
cold sleigh rides

Drawings of
Santa with
your family

Homemade Christmas
decorations for Mrs. Claus

Okay, now you know what you'll do once you catch Santa.
It's time to figure out HOW to do it. Definitely don't try
anything too WILD AND CRAZY:

Lassoing Santa

Distracting him with a giant candy cane

Luring him into a snow trap

Tying nets between palm trees

Instead: Be crafty! Be clever! Be *gentle*!

If you're very lucky, you will *actually catch Santa*. But you might only catch a *glimpse* of him. Or you might just find "Santa's been here" clues.

PLAN FOR ALL THESE POSSIBILITIES:

Early on Christmas Eve, write Santa a note and fill it with glitter.

When he opens it, glitter will sprinkle all over him and he'll leave a trail. That's a "Santa's been here" clue for sure.

Scatter carrots in your yard or on the windowsill.

If they disappear, that's a "reindeer have been here" clue!

Write Santa riddles, but
DON'T GIVE THE ANSWERS! (Yet.)

RIDDLES
?
FOR SANTA.

Bake him
cookies.

Instead of putting them
by the tree, draw arrows
leading to your room.

String bells and chimes
above the cookies.

That way, he'll make a
racket and wake you up.

Now try to be patient. While you wait, sing Christmas songs and read books about Santa. Maybe you'll even get some new Santa-catching ideas.

Ask your mom and dad if they ever tried to catch Santa when they were little. Do they have any tricks? Check with your grandma and grandpa, too.

When it starts to get dark, Santa and his reindeer begin
their rounds. Have everyone keep an eye out the window.

If your family makes lots of noise—laughing, eating,
talking, playing games—say "Shhhhh!" every now and
then and listen for Santa sounds. . . .

SANTA SOUNDS:

Santa doing stretches
on your neighbor's roof

Sleigh bells

"Ho, Ho, HO!"

Reindeer whinnying
in the distance

Elves giggling

When you start to get sleepy,
MAKE LAST-MINUTE PREPARATIONS:

Leave the Christmas tree lights on
to help Santa see his way around.

Rudolph-with-his-nose-so-bright can't help him from the roof.

Set out your Santa riddles with a note that says "For help with the answers, wake me up."

Santa won't be able to resist!

Is your puppy a good watchdog? A good, *gentle* watchdog? If yes, then let him stay in your bedroom.

Remember, Santa won't come to your house until you're asleep.

Before you lay your head on your pillow, peek out the window one last time.

Good luck catching Santa, and . . .

MERRY
CHRISTMAS!

And if you didn't catch Santa this time,
don't worry. There's always next year. . . .

SANTA
ROCKS

Thank You,
Santa, ♥
I wanted a pony
but I'm very
very happy with my
Doll's house.
Happy Christmas
♥   Love Eve

Hi, Santa
here is a picture
for you.

Thanks 4
my presents.

Thar
SAN
for gi
such
presen
see y
Year

To Santa,
you are the
best! Thank
you for my
new toy car.

To SANTA

THANK — YOU
P.S. I hope to catch you next year.